I Am God's Storyteller

WRITTEN BY
Lisa M. Hendey

ILLUSTRATED BY
Eric Carlson

PARACLETE PRESS
BREWSTER, MASSACHUSETTS

To all of the storytellers in my life, who have ignited in my heart a love
for God's magnificent imagination. Your stories have blessed me beyond measure and
have encouraged me to more boldly share my own.
—L.H.

For Lilian (and her big brothers, too).
—E.C.

I am God's storyteller. God imagined me at the dawn of all time for a very special mission: to help the world know his love.

Long before I was even a dream in my mother's and father's hearts, God gave me eyes to see, a heart to feel, a mind to ponder, and gifts and talents to share his stories in my own way.

God sent storytellers before me, to teach me the truth and to show me all the ways that God's stories could be shared.

When we tell God's stories, we storytellers help the world around us to know his love.

No storyteller is perfect. But we all love being part of God's storytelling mission.

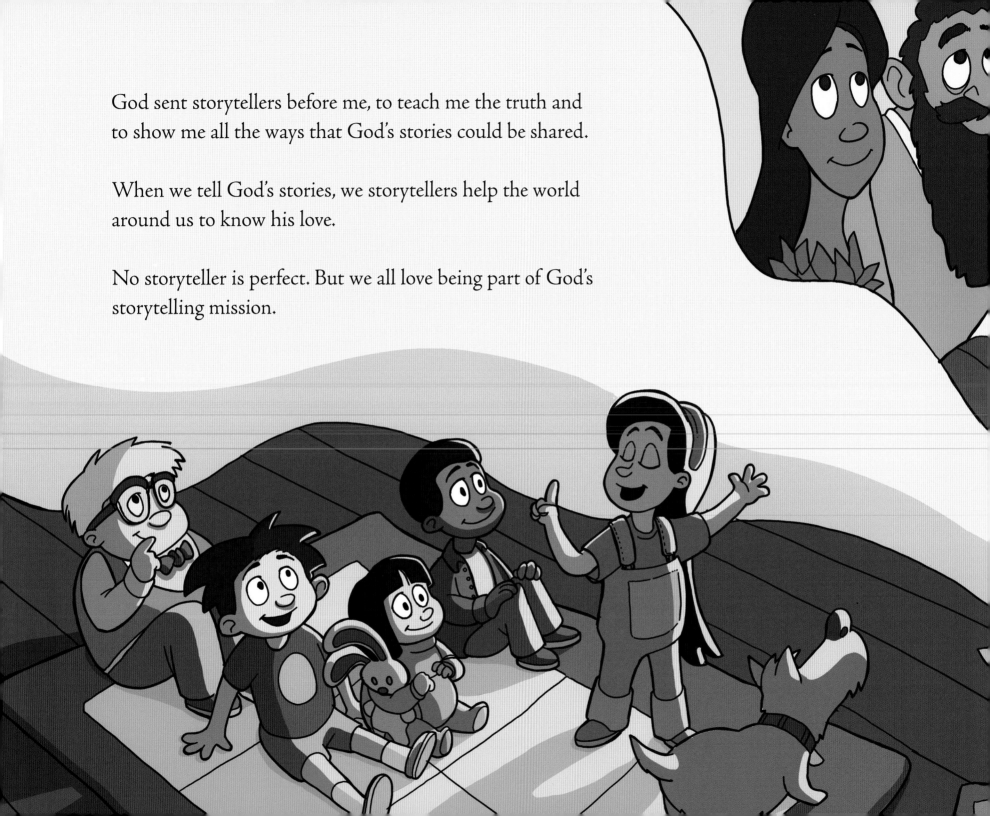

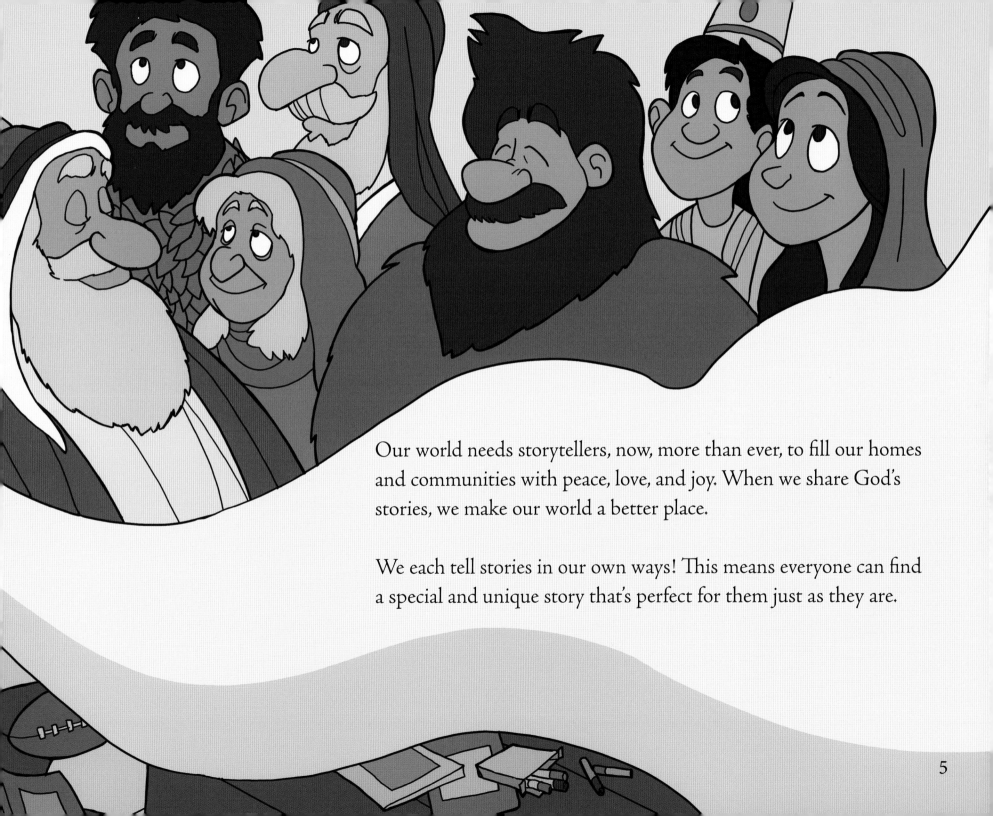

Our world needs storytellers, now, more than ever, to fill our homes and communities with peace, love, and joy. When we share God's stories, we make our world a better place.

We each tell stories in our own ways! This means everyone can find a special and unique story that's perfect for them just as they are.

In the beginning, God sent his first storytellers. But before they came, God created a world just waiting to hear their stories.

After he designed the heavens and the earth, God began our world's story with just a few words, whispering, "Let there be light." And there was light!

Next God created all we see around us: the sky, the land, the oceans, the sun, the moon, and the stars. God decorated the land with plants and trees and fruits and flowers to beautify our earth and to provide nutrition for us.

With so much beauty in our world, God created the fish and the birds and all kinds of beautiful animals to roam his creation.

Then came the most wonderful part of that very first story: God created man and woman, sending them to love and care for one another and for the rest of his creation. God gave them eyes to see, hearts to feel, minds to ponder, and special gifts and talents to share his stories in their own ways with their family.

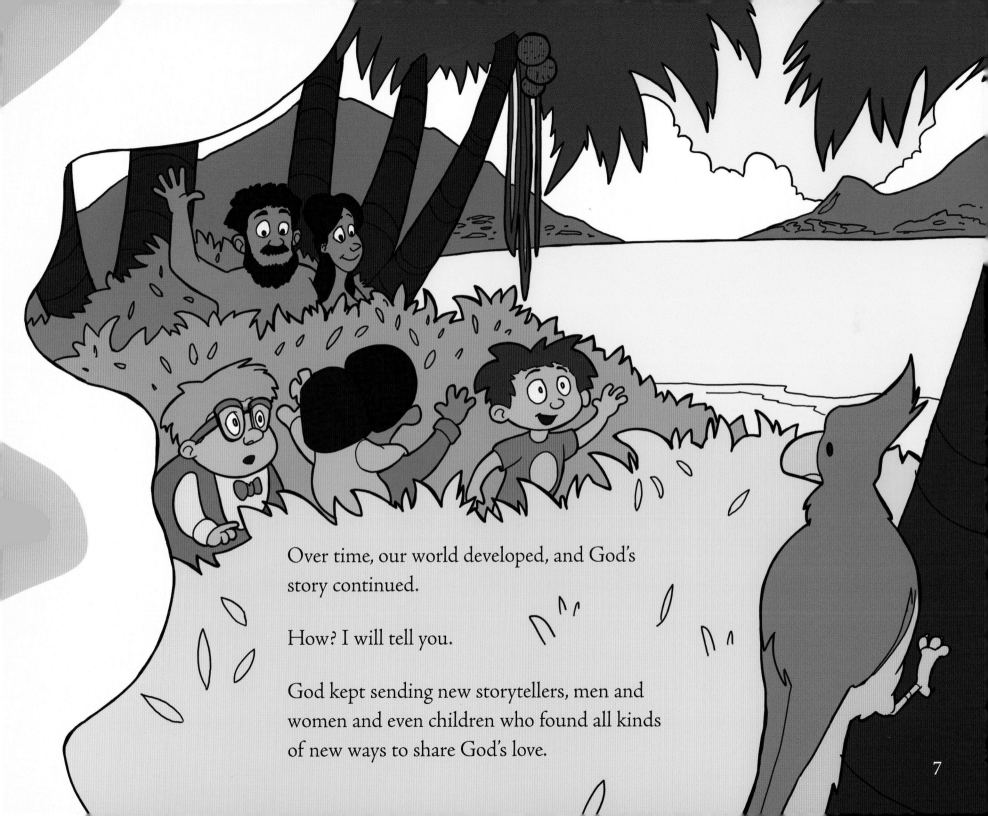

Over time, our world developed, and God's story continued.

How? I will tell you.

God kept sending new storytellers, men and women and even children who found all kinds of new ways to share God's love.

For instance, Sarah was a loving woman with a mother's heart. She longed to share her life with a child and to tell him all the stories inside her imagination. Along with her husband, Abraham, Sarah prayed for many years to become a mother.

Finally, when she was very, very old, Sarah gave birth to her precious son, Isaac. Sarah taught Isaac stories that helped him to become an important leader for his people.

Then, there was Moses. Do you know the story of Moses, and the essential story that Moses had to tell?

Moses lived a hard childhood in a country filled with anger and hurt, but God had a special mission in mind for him. Moses led God's people out of that country to safety. They wandered for many years until they found a new home. Along the way, Moses told his people many of God's stories!

High atop Mount Sinai, God gave Moses a special story to teach his people: important rules about how we should live with and love each other.

Moses was called a prophet, a special storyteller who received his story directly from God.

Deborah was a judge—a just, fair woman who helped her people make difficult decisions. The stories Deborah told with wisdom and faith in God helped God's people live peacefully together for many years.

Esther was a beautiful young woman who became a queen. She courageously told her stories to her king and helped to protect her kingdom!

David was a young boy who grew up to be a king, but he was also a great storyteller. David's "psalms" helped people to find a way to pray the feelings in their hearts.

There are so many stories God's people have told so far!

Isaiah lived in a challenging time and often had to tell his people stories that were hard to hear. He wanted people to know God's love, so he warned them that if they stopped following God's rules, their lives would be very hard.

Isaiah also promised his friends great hope: a special gift! His stories told the people of a Messiah, a savior, who would come as a sign of God's great love for them!

Then, there was Mary. You have to hear about Mary. She was one of God's greatest storytellers ever!

Even though she was still young, when God asked her to become the mother of his son, Jesus, Mary said, "Yes!"

In her home with Joseph, Mary taught little Jesus many stories. Mary also kept a lot of her stories very quiet, pondering them in her heart. Sometimes, I keep my stories quiet in my heart, too.

John the Baptist loved his relative, Jesus, so much and knew that Jesus was so special that John spent his whole life telling people stories about Jesus!

John told everyone he met about God's great love for them. He let them know that Jesus was coming and helped them prepare their hearts to welcome Jesus.

John wasn't afraid of anything!
Sometimes storytellers need to be brave.

Even as a young boy, Jesus loved learning about and telling his father God's stories.

Every year, Jesus would travel with Mary and Joseph to Jerusalem for the special festival of Passover. When Jesus was twelve, his parents were traveling home from the festival when suddenly, they realized that Jesus was not with any of their relatives. Jesus was lost! They hurried back to the temple in Jerusalem and found Jesus with the teachers, listening to their stories and asking them questions. Jesus reminded Mary and Joseph that he was God's beloved son. God had sent him into the world to teach us how to love one another.

Jesus' storytelling mission was almost ready to begin!

As the years passed, Jesus grew. When his storytelling mission was about to begin, he went into the desert for many days, opening his heart and mind to understand God's plan.

Next, Jesus invited special men to learn from him and journey with him. They were fishermen, business owners, a tax collector, and even a thief! Jesus called each of them to join him in sharing God's stories. Jesus knew that these men would each have a unique and special way of sharing God's love with the world.

Following Jesus wasn't always easy, but these men, Jesus' disciples, soon came to believe that Jesus was not only a special storyteller, but also the Son of God!

Jesus and the disciples traveled to new places to share God's stories. Jesus told his stories next to rivers and on top of mountains. He told them in big cities and small villages. He told his stories to people who already knew God and to people who were just learning about God for the very first time. Jesus told his stories to old people and to mothers and fathers and to good people and bad people, too.

Sometimes, people loved Jesus' stories and begged to hear more. At other times, Jesus' stories made people angry because Jesus wanted people to change and to live according to God's rules. Most of all, he wanted them to love each other.

When people refused to listen to his stories, Jesus left them and moved to a new place, meeting new friends along the way.

Jesus especially loved sharing stories with little children. He taught his disciples that God's kingdom belongs to everyone, especially children.

God certainly loves children in a special way. And everyone knows that children love to hear stories!

Some stories are real, and some stories are made up in our imaginations. Stories can teach us special lessons.

Jesus called some of his stories "parables." A parable is a special story with an important message. Jesus loved telling God's stories in parables because they were easier for his friends to understand and remember.

God loves us so very much that he sent his son,
Jesus, to be with us, to teach us God's stories, and
to help us discover how to share our own. After a
while, Jesus went to be with God in heaven. But
Jesus had so many wonderful friends who
wanted to keep sharing the stories
Jesus had taught them.

Have you heard about Peter, for instance, one of the most important early storytellers? Jesus' friend Peter started as one of the disciples. Then, Peter helped many to know and love the stories of Jesus.

Jesus was gone to heaven, but his stories never went away.

Many men and women began to pass them along. Mary Magdalene, Paul, Priscilla, Matthew, Mark, Luke, and John each had eyes to see, hearts to feel, minds to ponder, and special gifts and talents to share Jesus' stories in their own ways.

And they invited others to be storytellers, too.

Time passed, and the storytelling grew
and grew and grew!

21

Now it's OUR turn to be God's special storytellers.

We learn the stories from our parents, in our Bibles, and at our churches. We don't have to be grownups to be storytellers. Remember how much Jesus loved sharing his stories with children? As long as we have eyes to see, hearts to feel, and minds to ponder, we have everything we need to tell Jesus' stories in our own way!

22

I love to write my stories! I use big words and little ones and sometimes even make up my own words.

I picture the stories in my mind and then use my pencil, pen, crayons, or computer to share them.

Sometimes I just tell my stories out loud with my words.

My stories help my friends discover new worlds, new adventures, new characters, and new ways of knowing God's love.

I love to paint and sculpt and draw my stories!

I use brushes and clay and even my fingers to bring God's beauty to life.

My creations help people see the world differently. People can even touch and feel my stories!

I love to sing and dance my stories!

I use my feet and hands and voice to help people hear how much God loves us.

My songs have the power to make people act, to listen carefully, or to sing along as loud as they can. My dances help my friends want to dance for joy, too!

I love to play my stories!

I use cardboard and markers and sometimes even a computer to craft games to play with my friends.

My games help my friends to try their best, to play fairly, and to help their friends be good sports even when they aren't winning and want to quit!

I love to act and film my stories!

I use my body, my face, and sometimes even my mom and dad's camera. When I act my stories, I can be anyone, anywhere, at any time.

My imagination helps my friends be transported in time. My movies encourage them to daydream big, starry, action-packed adventures!

When I tell God's stories in any of these ways, my heart feels
closer to God and to the people I love.

Together, we learn, laugh, imagine, and dream.

I may be little, but I know that God made me especially for storytelling. And I know that our world needs my stories! Stories help us to understand each other and the world around us.

I've also learned something very important: To be a terrific storyteller, I must listen carefully to my friends' stories too! When I open my heart and listen to their stories, look at their pictures, sing their songs, or play their games, I learn even more about how much God loves me. And that makes me a better storyteller!

My stories are God's stories, told my way, with the imagination he gave especially to me, and the love he pours into each of us.

I am God's storyteller—and you are, too.

Let's go share his story of love today!

For Teachers, Parents, and Caregivers:

Thank you for encouraging the children in your care to embrace the art of storytelling. In my visits to schools around the country, I have learned that children not only love to hear great stories, but they also love to tell them! Here are a few ways to build a love for storytelling in your child's heart:

1. Share your family's stories early and often. Children are fascinated by lore and can learn from the way we relate our shared history.

2. Read voraciously to your children and encourage them to read. Read for pleasure as well as for learning. Let your child "catch" you reading just for fun. Read aloud, even after your child has learned to read.

3. Offer a variety of ways to encourage their storytelling. A journal can be as simple as an old recycled notebook. Kitchen pots and pans can be background instruments for an original song. Dance together, finger paint, look at the clouds and make up stories, or act out a new tale. Use an old cereal box to make a board game. Never stop imagining and don't place limits around your child's ability to create.

4. Unleash the power of your own stories. Set your imagination free to dream or research a period of history that fascinates you. Model your love for storytelling in your family.

5. Praise your child's efforts and dig deeper with questions. Offer feedback about how their story made you feel. Create emotional connections to what they have created and how their story can bless the world around them. Trust in the power of God's great love!

I pray that this book will be a blessing to you and your family. I can't wait to hear your child's stories. And I love visiting classrooms "virtually" and in person. So, if you would like to share a story with me or invite me, feel free to connect by email to lisa@lisahendey.com. May God instill in your home a true love for stories, and may those be an unending reminder of God's great love for you and your child.

Blessings,

Lisa

2019 First Printing

I Am God's Storyteller

Text copyright © 2019 Lisa M. Hendey
Illustrations copyright © 2019 by Eric Carlson

ISBN 978-1-64060-162-8

Library of Congress Cataloging-in-Publication Data is available.

10 9 8 7 6 5 4 3 2 1

Published by Paraclete Press
Brewster, Massachusetts
www.paracletepress.com

Printed in Korea by Prinpia